COMMUNITY CONNECTIONS

WHAT DOES IT DO?

FIRE TRUCK

BY JOSH GREGORY

Published in the United States of America by Cherry Lake Publishing
Ann Arbor, Michigan
www.cherrylakepublishing.com

Content Adviser: Louis Teel, Professor of Heavy Equipment, Central Arizona College
Reading Adviser: Cecilia Minden-Cupp, PhD, Literacy Consultant

Photo Credits: Cover and page 1, ©Msavoia/Dreamstime.com; page 5, ©James Steidl/Dreamstime.com; page 7, ©Denise Kappa/Shutterstock, Inc.; page 9, ©Condor 36/Shutterstock, Inc.; page 11, ©Pyroshot/Dreamstime.com; page 13, ©Monkey Business Images/Dreamstime.com; page 15, ©Mike Brake/Shutterstock, Inc.; page 17, ©Phartisan/Dreamstime.com; page 19, ©Eric Inghels/Dreamstime.com; page 21, ©Angela Farley/Shutterstock, Inc.

LIBRARY OF CONGRESS CATALOGING-IN-PUBLICATION DATA
Gregory, Josh.
What does it do? Fire truck/by Josh Gregory.
p. cm.—(Community connections)
Includes bibliographical references and index.
ISBN-13: 978-1-60279-971-4 (lib. bdg.)
ISBN-10: 1-60279-971-7 (lib. bdg.)
1. Fire engines—Juvenile literature. I. Title. II. Title: Fire truck. III. Series.
TH9372.G74 2011
628.9'259—dc22 2010023585

Cherry Lake Publishing would like to acknowledge the work of The Partnership for 21st Century Skills. Please visit *www.21stcenturyskills.org* for more information.

Printed in the United States of America
Corporate Graphics Inc.
January 2011
CLSP08

FIRE TRUCK

CONTENTS

A BUILDING IS ON FIRE!

Oh, no! The old building down the street is on fire! What can we do? It's time to call the fire department. **Firefighters** will come to put out the fire.

Firefighters work hard to put out fires.

Firefighters at the station nearby get the call about the fire. A fire bell rings. The firefighters put on their uniforms. The uniforms help protect them.

Then the firefighters get in the fire truck. They turn on the **sirens**. It's time to fight the fire!

Fire trucks leave the station within minutes of a call.

LOOK!

Have you ever seen your town's fire department? Ask a parent to take you to see it. You might get to see some fire trucks parked outside!

PUTTING OUT THE FLAMES

Fire trucks have **hoses** that spray water. Firefighters use the hoses to help put out fires. The hoses can spray water very far.

It takes a lot of water to put out a big fire. Where does the water come from?

Hoses come in different sizes.

Some fire trucks get their water from fire **hydrants**. You may have seen a hydrant on your street.

Hydrants are bright colors, such as red or yellow. Firefighters use hoses to connect fire trucks to hydrants.

What color are the fire hydrants in your neighborhood?

THINK!

Fire hydrants are painted bright colors. You can spot them almost anywhere you go. Why do you think hydrants are bright colors? Why are there so many?

Other fire trucks store water in **tanks**. They don't need hydrants. The tanks take up a lot of space in the fire trucks.

Sometimes fire trucks get water from lakes or ponds. Firefighters use **pumps** to suck water into the tanks.

Driving a fire truck is different from driving a car.

FIRE
WHEEL LOCK

Firefighters also use foam to put out fires. The foam keeps the fire from starting again. Fire trucks carry the foam to where it is needed.

Other fire trucks have water cannons. Cannons shoot water out faster than fire hoses. Firefighters use water cannons to put out big fires.

Water cannons can quickly shoot out a lot of water.

AIR
AIR

A fire truck has many smaller tools, too. **Axes** help clear the way into burning buildings. **Wrenches** are used to connect hoses to hydrants.

Fire trucks hold axes and other supplies.

Some fire trucks have long ladders. Firefighters use them to reach the windows of tall buildings. They can rescue people who are trapped on the high floors.

Firefighters can also spray water from the ladders. This helps put out fires on the tops of buildings.

Some ladders have buckets at the end that help firefighters reach high places.

A JOB WELL DONE

The firefighters have worked hard. The fire truck's tools have helped them put out the fire. The people in the building are safe.

Now you know what fire trucks do. Firefighters could not put out fires without them!

Sometimes fire trucks take part in parades.

ASK QUESTIONS!

Do you know any firefighters? If not, ask your parents if you can meet some. Ask the firefighters how they learned to use a fire truck. They can also tell you more about a fire truck's many tools.

GLOSSARY

axes (AK-siz) sharp tools used to chop things apart

firefighters (FYR-fye-turz) people who work to put out fires

hoses (HOHZ-iz) long tubes used to spray water or to suck water into tanks on fire trucks

hydrants (HYE-druhntss) outdoor pipes that supply water that is used to fight fires

pumps (PUHMPSS) devices that move water from one place to another

sirens (SYE-ruhnz) objects that make a loud noise in order to warn people of danger

tanks (TANGKSS) large containers for holding water

wrenches (RENCH-iz) tools used to tighten or loosen something

FIND OUT MORE

BOOKS

Coppendale, Jean. *Fire Trucks and Rescue Vehicles*. Laguna Hills, CA: QEB Publishing, 2007.

Gordon, Sharon. *What's Inside a Fire Truck*. New York: Marshall Cavendish Benchmark, 2007.

Lindeen, Mary. *Fire Trucks*. Minneapolis: Bellwether Media, 2007.

WEB SITES

Fire Engine Photos
www.fire-engine-photos.com/
See pictures of many different kinds of fire engines.

HowStuffWorks—How Fire Engines Work
science.howstuffworks.com/fire-engine.htm
Learn about the different parts of fire engines.

Sparky.org—Fire Truck Home Page
www.sparky.org/firetruck/index.htm
Look at pictures on this fun Web site, and learn more about fire trucks.

INDEX

ABOUT THE AUTHOR

Josh Gregory writes and edits books for kids. He lives in Chicago, Illinois.